# *Hea*



*We Die...*

*What happens after we take our last breath?*

**Jody Patrick Miller**

**Pastor and Missionary**

For more books, visit my site on Amazon:

https://www.amazon.com/s?k=jody+patrick+miller&ref=nb_sb_noss

3rd Edition, published October 2023

*Acknowledgments*

Special thanks to all my friends and family members who helped in bringing this story to life, especially my daughter Cathy, and my beautiful wife Ruth.

*Cover Photo*

By KDP

All scripture quotations are from the New King James Version of the Bible, Thomas Nelson Publishers

Book Format 5x8

# Contents

# *Heaven* Five Seconds *After We Die...*

## Introduction

Is there anyone alive that hasn't wondered about the afterlife? What happens when we die? Do the lights just go off? Do we cease to exist? Or is there something more?

For those that have no personal relationship with Jesus, this will be a terrifying day. Beware!

But for Christians, there will be no terror but joy! We know that Heaven awaits, but many questions remain. When we die do we "sleep" until the resurrection, or do we go directly to Heaven?

We leave our old broken-down bodies behind, but then what? Do we become ghosts, with no physical bodies?

When we get to Heaven, will we see our loved ones, and will we know them?

Will we eat and drink? Will we be married to our former spouse and live together in the same house?

Find out the answers to these questions and more, plus what's up next on the heavenly calendar.

# The Rain

Rachel stood up, walked to the window, and drew the blinds. In the light of the street lights, she could see the drizzle had turned to a steady rain. Maybe if she went outside and let the rain fall on her face, she could clear her head. Closing her eyes and tilting her head back she could almost feel it. Then she began to cry, again.

Dad loved the rain. She walked over to his bed and gently took his hand. It was warm, reassuring her he was still alive. "Dad, it's raining," she said softly. She almost asked "Do you want to go for a walk?" but she didn't. The sad fact was her dad was not going to be walking, not in the rain, nor anywhere else. Would he ever feel the rain on his face ever again?

She wiped a tear and returned to her chair. Looking up a few minutes later, she noticed he was awake. She stood up and looked at him, but didn't say anything. Every time she did, she started crying and it ended with him comforting her.

"Could you get my Bible please?" he croaked. His once booming voice was now barely a whisper, and even that seemed to take a lot of effort.

He told her to turn to First Thessalonians 5:16. Putting her finger on the verse, that had been highlighted and underlined, she looked up. He nodded and she read:

"REJOICE ALWAYS, PRAY WITHOUT CEASING, IN EVERYTHING GIVE THANKS; FOR THIS IS THE WILL OF GOD IN CHRIST JESUS FOR YOU."

He pointed to her and gave her a weak smile. She managed a half smile of her own.

He asked her to turn to Second Corinthians Chapter 5.

"FOR WE KNOW THAT IF OUR EARTHLY HOUSE, *THIS* TENT, IS DESTROYED, WE HAVE A BUILDING FROM GOD, A HOUSE NOT MADE WITH HANDS, ETERNAL IN THE HEAVENS.

FOR IN THIS WE GROAN, EARNESTLY DESIRING TO BE CLOTHED WITH OUR HABITATION WHICH IS FROM HEAVEN, IF INDEED, HAVING BEEN CLOTHED, WE SHALL NOT BE FOUND NAKED.

FOR WE WHO ARE IN *THIS* TENT GROAN, BEING BURDENED, NOT BECAUSE WE WANT TO BE UNCLOTHED, BUT FURTHER CLOTHED, THAT MORTALITY MAY BE

SWALLOWED UP BY LIFE.

NOW HE WHO HAS PREPARED US FOR THIS VERY THING *IS* GOD, WHO ALSO HAS GIVEN US THE SPIRIT AS A GUARANTEE.

SO *WE ARE* ALWAYS CONFIDENT, KNOWING THAT WHILE WE ARE AT HOME IN THE BODY WE ARE ABSENT FROM THE LORD.

FOR WE WALK BY FAITH, NOT BY SIGHT.

She stopped, thinking this was the end, but he motioned for her to keep reading.

"WE ARE CONFIDENT, YES, WELL PLEASED."

As she read the word "confident" he nodded. At "well pleased" he nodded again. She stopped and asked, "So, you are well pleased?" She was thinking to herself, "You're dying, how can you be 'pleased'?!" But he was motioning for her to finish the verse.

"TO BE ABSENT FROM THE BODY AND TO BE PRESENT WITH THE LORD."

At this, he gave an emphatic nod.

"I get it Dad; you are longing to leave this body (with its pain and suffering) and to be with Jesus."

He nodded but motioned for her to turn the Bible around. She thought he wanted to read himself but he said weakly, "No, you, turn the verse around." At this, he exhaled deeply and closed his eyes, apparently exhausted from the effort of the conversation.

An hour or more passed and his breathing seemed to be slower. She picked up a brochure from the table titled "How to Know When the End Is Near." She thought to herself, "First clue: you are reading this brochure." She put it back down.

Sarah arrived at about nine, to give her a break. Rachel had sent her home the night before to put the kids to bed and get some sleep. "Hey sis, sorry I'm late, the kids missed the bus and I had to drive them. Any news?"

She gave her little sister a hug, and a quick update, before rushing out. If she hurried, she could get home, do some laundry, and bring lunch back to the Hospice Center. Dashing back in she said, "Italian, Mexican, or burgers?"

Sarah shook her head sadly. "I can't even think of food, but thanks for asking."

At 12:10, the drive-thru line at Wendy's reached all the way to the street. Maybe she should have ordered inside? But she was boxed in now so nothing to do but wait. Suddenly her hands started to tingle and her heart fluttered. What's up with that? She took her hands off the wheel and took a few deep breaths. Fatigue. And stress. A good hot meal would help. A bowl of mom's chicken soup would be wonderful, but Mom was gone, and her chicken soup. And now dad...

A horn beeped behind her, making her jump. Three more cars between her and the order station. Two hot bowls of chili should breathe a little life into her, and Sarah. She had to take care of Sarah, it's what big sisters do.

The tone sounded on the elevator and the doors opened. Tuning down the hallway she saw Sarah coming toward her, and she knew something was wrong. She set off towards her with a purposeful stride. Sarah met her and said, "I'm sorry, Sis, I tried to call you..."

Rachel looked at her, accusation in her eyes. Funny her phone hadn't rung. "Sarah, what did you do?"

Sarah looked confused. Rachel headed toward the room and Sarah grabbed her hand. "I'm sorry, Sis, he's gone."

"No, he's not, I was just talking to him," Rachel said jerking her hand away.

"Rachel, don't."

Rushing in, she saw her dad's body, the hospice nurse gently placing a towel under his head. "Your dad didn't suffer; he just went to sleep."

"When?" asked Rachel.

The nurse glanced at the whiteboard, where someone had written "T O D 12:10 pm"

Rachel looked at the whiteboard, then at her father's body lying motionless on the bed, and the room began to spin.

# Earlier That Morning…

William Hardy had a strange feeling. The dull throbbing pain was tempered by the euphoric high from the painkillers. He hated drugs, but he hated pain more, so he had relented. He heard Rachel say, "It's raining, Dad" and he immediately began looking for his raincoat. But it was missing. He looked down the hall and the entire coat tree was missing. He was confused but not really bothered. Somehow, he knew that soon he'd have no need for coats and scarves, toboggans, or gloves. The cold was something this earthly body felt, but when he left this body, he'd no longer be cold. Nor hot. Nor would he be sick. No arthritis, no headaches, no cancer. Hallelujah!

He looked around his house, at all the treasures he and his wife had collected. In the garage were his tools, his car, his lawnmower, and his weed eater. No weeds in Heaven, he was certain.

His house and belongings began to fade, and he realized he would no longer need any of them. And he wouldn't miss any of it – he would be exchanging the mere trinkets of this world for all the riches of glory. For when he received Jesus as Lord and Savior, Jesus had received him, as a brother. And he had become a joint heir with the King of Kings. Hallelujah!

So, was this it? Was he leaving now? Certainly, he was ready. Ready to see his dear wife again, to see his mother and father, grandparents, and many friends, all gone on before him. But most of all, first of all, and most important of all, he wanted to see his Lord and Savior. The one who gave everything, even His own life, so that his sins could be paid for.

He was ready. But there was one thing holding him back: Rachel. Rachel was the organizer, the planner, the big sister, and the caretaker. She took care of everything and everyone. Everyone that is except herself.

Sarah was different. She was a free spirit. She'd sit in the tall grass, oblivious to its wetness or the possible grass stains on her clothes. She'd hold out her hand, hoping a butterfly would land there. And sometimes it did, in which case she'd talk softly to it, and hold out her hand for as long as the butterfly chose to stay.

They would mourn his death, as they had mourned their mother's death. Sarah would, he was sure, accept death as a part of life. It would be hard but she would incorporate it into who she is and move on, stronger and wiser. And she had her husband and two little boys. Their lives were wrapped up in church. Gary was a deacon and Sarah stayed busy working in the nursery, organizing bake sales, and leading a church drama team.

Both were strong believers, thankfully. They had their faith in Christ to anchor them, but their personalities were different. Sarah spent very little time planning and zero time worrying. She just went on her merry way and everything seemed to work itself out.

Rachel tried to manage everything and plan everything, yet her plans often failed, leaving her disappointed.

William opened his eyes and slowly took in his surroundings, realizing he wasn't dead, and saddened by the fact. His first tentative steps into the afterlife had been so sweet, so warm and inviting. He had stood at the threshold of Heaven and was overjoyed with the prospect of stepping across. He literally wished he were dead!

But like the Apostle Paul, who said he preferred to go on to Heaven, but it was necessary that he stay and be a help to others, he had to return. He saw Rachel, saw and felt her pain. More than anything he wanted her to be happy, to experience real joy.

He prayed that the Holy Spirit would guide him, one more time, in giving the right word, a "WORD SPOKEN IN DUE SEASON". 1st Thessalonians 5:17 came to mind. He wished he'd spent more time memorizing scripture, and the references. He knew the verse he wanted, but was that the right reference? As soon as she started reading, he knew it was the right verse. He smiled and saw Rachel smile as well. "Thank you, God."

Now, about my departing. I want her to understand that I'm not actually dying, that this body is just a temporary dwelling place. Like Paul said, "it is a tent." Tents are temporary, never designed to last forever. Our souls, on the other hand, were designed to live forever. When our "tent" wears out, it begins to leak. Tears open up which let in the wind. It begins to mold, and the bottom rots. The ropes begin to give way, and the stakes rot and break off. Lastly, the poles give way and the whole thing collapses. At this point, it is thrown on the trash heap and discarded.

This body we live in is our home here on earth, and we do our best to take care of it and make it last as long as possible. And we are thankful for it, but at the same time, we believers long to be with the Lord. And we eventually realize that this body actually prevents us from being with the Lord.

Like an old car with many miles on it, our bodies sometimes break down. Medical science is able to fix many of these breakdowns, but not all, and not forever. As we get older, our bodies no longer function like they did when we were younger. Disease and decay become more evident and we suffer pain and disability.

But the good news is all physical pain, all disease, and all disabilities, are all connected to our bodies, so when we leave our bodies, we, by definition, leave these illnesses behind. Hallelujah!

Even our brains are part of our physical bodies. All mental illnesses, depression, psychoses, and all addictions will also be left behind. Double Hallelujah!

It gets better and better. The sin, which hounds us our entire lives, is also connected to our bodies. That's in Romans 7. All the self-centeredness, petty jealousies, and our propensity to do wrong when we want to do right, are all connected to the body, so once again, when we leave our bodies, we leave our sinful desires and temptations. Hallelujah! Hallelujah! Hallelujah!

# In the Break Room

Rachel awakened to see her sister standing over her with a worried look on her face. Daisy, the hospice nurse was wiping her face with a wet washcloth.

"You gave us quite a scare, Sis," said Sarah, "thankfully Daisy caught you before you hit the floor."

"Wh-What happened?" asked Rachel weakly.

"Seen it happen many-a-time," said Daisy in her South Carolina accent, "you just got KO'd by a whole lotta stress. Too much stress, too little sleep..."

"And too little food", added Sarah.

Right on cue, the microwave went "beep beep beep."

Sarah brought over the two bowls of Wendy's chili, freshly reheated.

"Really I can't eat a thing," protested Rachel.

"Doctor's orders," said Daisy, and added "and lots of water."

Rachel started to get up but Sarah and Daisy pushed her back down. "Let me be the big sister for a while. You've been through a lot Sis; you need to take a time out."

After finishing the chili, Rachel did feel much better. "So, tell me what happened."

Slowly, painfully, Sarah began. "After you left Dad just slept, but then his breathing got real shallow." I called the nurse and she checked his pulse and said 'it won't be long now.' I wanted to call you, Sis, but then his breathing got shallower, then it just stopped."

# At 12:10 PM

William Hardy found himself at the front door of his house. He opened the door, expecting to find his wife, Linda, inside. Linda means "beautiful" and they'd called their property "Loma Linda" (beautiful hill). He hoped he could live in this beautiful house with his beautiful wife throughout all eternity.

But what he found was a moving crew, busily packing. The two recliners where he and his wife used to watch TV, were wrapped in shrink wrap. He heard the rattle of dishes from the kitchen. He searched the whole house hoping he'd find his wife, but deep down he knew he wouldn't. His bed had been dismantled and the mattress and box springs were propped against the wall.

"Well," he said to himself, "it was a nice thought, but really we always knew this wouldn't be our home forever." As a pastor, he'd preached sermons entitled "Our Citizenship Is in Heaven" and "Though We Live Here This Is Not Our Home." He loved songs like Beulah Land which says "I'm kinda homesick for a country, where I've never been before."

He was homesick for Heaven and had been for a long, long time. Now, it seemed he was on the brink. What would it be like? He crossed through the kitchen and into the garage. There sat his candy apple red and white 57 Chevy, just as he'd left it. The paint job was beautiful. But it had no seats, the wheels and rims were stacked in the corner and the carburetor and a bunch of the engine parts were in cardboard boxes. If this were Heaven that car would be all put together and running. He smiled and wished the new owner good luck.

Suddenly the room started to dim as it did before when he went back to comfort Rachel. He looked behind him and he saw his room at the hospice. He saw his own body lying on the bed and two nurses checking his vital signs. He saw Sarah looking on in concern.

Was he going back? In his spirit he heard a voice say, "No son, your work on earth is over. Your pain and suffering are finished. Heaven awaits."

He turned away from the hospice room and walked forward. He stopped at the garage door. He attempted to push the door open, and to his surprise, he walked right through it.

# At the Table

"What ya writin' Sis?", asked Sarah.

"Huh? Oh... I was just planning out the funeral. Thinking of Dad's favorite songs, any ideas?"

"No, actually I wanted to ask you if Dad talked to you before he uh..."

"Died? Yes, he did, early this morning before you came."

"What did you guys talk about?"

Sarah retrieved her dad's Bible and Rachel showed her the verses they'd read.

"TO BE ABSENT FROM THE BODY IS TO BE PRESENT WITH THE LORD."

What do you think he meant by "turn the verse around?", asked Rachel.

"Try this," said Sarah "what if we read it this way:

'TO BE PRESENT WITH THE LORD IS TO BE ABSENT FROM THE BODY?'"

That would mean we can't be with the Lord without leaving our bodies."

"Hum," mused Rachel, "that would make

sense since our bodies are corrupt and God cannot stand in the presence of sin. But does that mean dad is floating around with no body? Like a ghost?"

"God gave him a new body?" suggested Sarah.

"Well..." Rachel started, "look back at verse one."

"FOR WE KNOW THAT IF OUR EARTHLY HOUSE, *THIS* TENT, IS DESTROYED, WE HAVE A BUILDING FROM GOD, A HOUSE NOT MADE WITH HANDS, ETERNAL IN THE HEAVENS."

"If I'm understanding that verse, it says that Dad swapped his tent for a building."

"That's cool." Said Sarah, thinking of their camping trips and their old leaky moldy tent. "Sounds like dad got an upgrade."

"Big time," Rachel agreed "he traded an army surplus tent for a condo built by God."

Sarah put her hand on her chest because it really was painful when she laughed – she didn't realize how tense she was. "He traded something temporary for something permanent."

"Yes, he took off mortality and put on immortality."

Sarah smiled, "So dad finally has his resurrection body."

"Uh no, I don't think so," said Rachel. "The resurrection hasn't happened yet, remember, 'The dead in Christ shall rise first,' that's just before the rapture."

"So unless the rapture just happened and we missed it?" said Sarah with a sly grin.

"Well in that case it's a good thing I stopped by the ATM."

They both laughed this time, just a little, but it felt good. Truly laughter is the best medicine.

Rachel flipped over to 1st Thessalonians 4.

"BUT I DO NOT WANT YOU TO BE IGNORANT, BRETHREN, CONCERNING THOSE WHO HAVE FALLEN ASLEEP, LEST YOU SORROW AS OTHERS WHO HAVE NO HOPE.

FOR IF WE BELIEVE THAT JESUS DIED AND ROSE AGAIN, EVEN SO GOD WILL BRING WITH HIM THOSE WHO SLEEP IN JESUS.

FOR THIS WE SAY TO YOU BY THE WORD OF THE LORD, THAT WE WHO ARE ALIVE AND REMAIN UNTIL THE COMING OF THE LORD

WILL BY NO MEANS PRECEDE THOSE WHO ARE ASLEEP.

FOR THE LORD HIMSELF WILL DESCEND FROM HEAVEN WITH A SHOUT, WITH THE VOICE OF AN ARCHANGEL, AND WITH THE TRUMPET OF GOD. AND THE DEAD IN CHRIST WILL RISE FIRST.

THEN WE WHO ARE ALIVE AND REMAIN SHALL BE CAUGHT UP TOGETHER WITH THEM IN THE CLOUDS TO MEET THE LORD IN THE AIR. AND THUS WE SHALL ALWAYS BE WITH THE LORD.

THEREFORE COMFORT ONE ANOTHER WITH THESE WORDS."

Sarah rubbed her chin. "I always wondered about that word 'sleep,' is that talking about 'Soul Sleep'? I'm not sure what that is, to be honest."

"That's the belief that when believers die, they don't go straight to Heaven, rather they go to a place where they 'sleep' until the resurrection. These verses seem to support that but in reality, the word sleep is just a euphemism for dying. The other passage we read in Second Corinthians makes it crystal clear that to be absent from the body is to be present with the Lord. There's another passage in Philippians where Paul says he is hard-pressed between his desire to stay here and bear fruit and his desire to depart and be with Christ."

Sarah asked her sister, "Isn't Soul Sleep like a cult thing?"

Rachel replied, "I'm no expert, but I think the Seventh Day Adventists and the Jehovah's Witnesses are the ones that believe in it. But there are others including part of the Lutherans. As I understand it, it was Martin Luther himself who started the idea." Even some popular songs we sing in church weave in this idea of a "slumbering place" where we sleep until the resurrection.

"But what did Jesus say?" asked Sarah.

"What did He tell the thief on the cross?" Rachel queried.

"He said 'Today, you will be with me in paradise.'"

In the hallway, there was the sound of a gurney rolling by. Both turned to look and outside the glass window they saw a body on the gurney, the sheet pulled tight over the face and head.

"Oh, God, no!" shouted Rachel, gripping Sarah's arm like a vise.

"Rachel, calm down, that's not Dad. Didn't you just say that he's with the Lord?"

## At 12:10 PM, Five Seconds After William Hardy Died

Out in the driveway, everything seemed to be bathed in a white glow, like a fog, but it was warm and bright. What could it be? Then he realized, this is God. God is everywhere, all the time. On earth, he couldn't see God but now he could. Praise God forever and ever! He remembered a verse:

"AND THUS WE SHALL ALWAYS BE WITH THE LORD."

Praise God, Praise God, Praise God! He was in Heaven! He had no pain, for the first time in years, and he was walking around and had a spring in his step.

He really felt good. He stretched out his arms and flexed his hands. He realized his hands were different. Gone were those embarrassing liver spots – these were the hands of a young man. And his arms were strong and muscular. His forearms and his biceps were, well to put it in modern slang, he was "ripped!" He'd worked out as a young man but had not been too successful with it. Then as he got older, around 30 he put on a few pounds, at 40 a few more, at 50 a smidge more. Then cancer and the chemo and radiation had just about destroyed him.

He began to laugh. "I thought in Heaven I'd be like I was at 22 years of age, basically a younger, healthier version of myself, but this is insane." He remembered the words of Jesus, "UNLESS A SEED FALLS TO THE GROUND AND DIES..." Then the new plant cannot be born.

Then he remembered another verse from First Corinthians talking about the same thing. A seed falling to the earth and dying. And that seed comes back to life. Paul says in 1st Corinthians 15:38:

"BUT GOD GIVES IT A BODY AS HE PLEASES, AND TO EACH SEED ITS OWN BODY."

Feeling the muscles on his chest and admiring his nice flat stomach he remarked "A body of God's own choosing? Well done, God, very well done. Thank you."

He walked over to the huge stone at the end of his driveway. "Let's see if I can move it." He remembered how much work it had been for him and Linda to move it. And that was with his pickup truck and chains and a pry bar. He bent over the rock and moved it from side to side to break it loose from the ground. He squatted beside it, wrapped his arms around it, and to his surprise, picked it up like a sack of potatoes. Careful not to drop it on his toes, he dropped it, then he threw his head back and laughed. "Who would have believed it? Not in my wildest dreams."

He felt so good. He was healthier and far stronger than he had ever been on earth. "I believe I'm taller too." He started towards the garage to compare his height to the garage door, but to his surprise, the garage and the whole house were gone. "That's fine, I knew that was coming. I'm glad actually, that thing was a maintenance nightmare."

In its place was a lush forest with tall trees and flowers and ferns and a picturesque stream flowing through the middle. An inviting path followed the course of the stream. He began walking upstream. It was one of those Indian Summer days that you dream about, perfect in every way.

"I wonder if there are animals," William thought to himself, and at just that moment a doe wandered onto the path just ahead of him. Shyly, a little fawn nudged its head around its mother.

William was very still, not wanting to spook her. He waited a long time and finally, he felt he had to move. Slowly he walked toward her, at any moment expecting her to bolt away, her white flag tail waving a warning to other deer. To his surprise, she never ran. He walked up to her, patted her on the head, and rubbed her ears. The fawn nudged his hands wanting his share of the attention. "God, don't let me wake up and find that this was only a dream."

Moving on, the sound of the water became louder and louder, and turning a corner he spotted a waterfall. Not the tallest he'd seen but definitely the most beautiful. The water came over the top and separated from the cliff face before hitting another rock. This produced a large volume of spray and the light passing through created not a rainbow (since the light was coming from all directions) but a kaleidoscope of color all around. He raised his hands above his head and praised God.

Up ahead he noticed a lone figure dressed in white. It was a woman with long blonde hair, seated on a rock facing the waterfall. There was only one person in all the universe that could be. "Linda!"

he yelled. She turned and smiled as she watched him running towards her. He ran fast and hard but when he arrived he was not out of breath. He stood looking at her serene face, with tiny drops of water from the mist trickling down her cheeks, surrounded by an aura of multicolored light. It was the most beautiful thing he had ever seen. He didn't know whether to shake hands or to wrap her in his arms and kiss her. In the end, he said, "Hi."

"Hi yourself, it took you long enough," she replied with a mischievous smirk.

"Well, I was at the house, our house, and I went outside and there was light all around, and you know that big rock at the end of the driveway? I picked that thing up! By myself!"

Meanwhile, Linda stood by smiling with her hand on her chin. She was so beautiful.

"Can I have a hug?" she asked shyly.

He squeezed her so hard he was afraid he'd hurt her. He rubbed her back and thought to himself, "She is actually real. Not a ghost, not a dream." Then he started crying and she cried too.

Finally, she rubbed her eyes and said, "I've been waiting so long for you to come."

"Yes, well, when you had your accident, well, I thought I would die. I never told anyone, but I actually considered suicide. It was just so hard. For the girls too. But every time one of us would hit bottom, the others would be there. And you know what? There were many times when God would send someone to help us, at just the right time."

Linda touched his arm. "I know. And I'd like to think that I helped you during those times."

"You mean? What do you mean? Are you an Angel?"

Linda laughed and covered her mouth. "No, I'm not an Angel. But I am like an Angel. And so are you."

William was puzzled, "So what do you do?"

Linda smiled, "Well, mostly we worship and we work."

William lit up. "Amen to that. I was hoping to have work to do."

"Well, you won't be disappointed. We

have lots of work, important work. We're not guardian angels like some people think. We're not Angels, but we do help the Angels, we're part of a team."

"So, we're teammates then, you and I?", asked William, a little confused.

Linda saw his confusion and sought to reassure him. "I know this is a lot to take in, but don't worry, I'm not going anywhere." She knew he wanted to know what their relationship was now that they were no longer on earth.

She invited him to sit beside her. "Do you remember the story of the wife who married seven brothers?"

"Yes, I remember it well, it's in Matthew, Mark, and Luke. But you never hear about it in church, I guess it makes people uncomfortable," replied William.

Linda continued, "Well the Sadducees used it to try to trick Jesus, but it was a true story and Jesus responded in a way that silenced them and also taught a valuable lesson about the afterlife. If people are uncomfortable with his answer, they should examine themselves. Jesus told the Sadducees they were in error, maybe they are too."

William was thinking about the story. "The tradition of that day was that if a man died childless, it was his brother's duty to marry his widow and produce an heir for his dead brother. But in this case, all seven married her, one by one, all died and no children were produced. Finally, the woman died."

Linda nodded. "It's natural for people to assume life in Heaven is the same as it is on earth, just a little nicer. It never occurs to them that the natural order of things might be different."

William looked down, suddenly feeling uneasy. "I've had a lot of people ask me about what Jesus said, and to be honest with you I wasn't sure what to tell them. Jesus said that in Heaven they neither marry nor are given in marriage but are like the Angels in Heaven."

Linda looked at William with tenderness and compassion. "William, I know what you are thinking and what you want to ask me. When we met and fell in love, I promised to love you forever, and I am keeping that promise. William, I will always love you, but with a stronger more perfect, more mature kind of love than was ever possible before. Our love will be different because we are different. Our love will be better because we are better. On earth, all our relationships were tainted by sin. Here that's not the case."

William nodded beginning to understand. "Well, amen to that, like Paul said 'wretched man that I am! Who will deliver me from this body of death?' By the way, will I see Paul?"

Linda was nodding, "And Matthew, Mark, Luke, and John. Don't get in any hurry, you'll have all of eternity to talk to them."

William was excited, "I have so many questions."

Linda was smiling, "I knew you'd finally be happy. I will see you again soon, but for now, I have something urgent I need to attend to down on earth."

"Rachel and Sarah?" asked William.

Linda nodded.

William asked, "Can you remind them how much I love them? And tell them not to worry about me? And tell Rachel not to worry and to try to be happy?"

"I will do my best," said Linda. She was sure that William had no idea of the nature of their work, but it was after all his first day in Heaven.

"One last hug before I go."

As she was leaving her appearance began to change, and then she just disappeared.

# It's the Lord

As he turned to go, he saw someone skipping rocks on the pool at the bottom of the waterfall. Though this person had their back to him he knew... Jesus! He ran quickly and stood beside him. Jesus smiled at him and handed him a rock. When he saw the nail prints on Jesus' hand, he literally stopped breathing.

Jesus threw his rock and it skipped four times before sinking into the water.

Awkwardly William threw his rock at the top of the pool. "Plaap" went the rock, straight into the water. Too hard obviously, seems he didn't know his own strength.

Jesus motioned for him to watch him throw. He bent low and threw the rock like a baseball with a lot of spin on it. It skipped five times before sinking.

William threw, copying Jesus' example, and his rock skipped four times.

Jesus clapped his hands and said, "Well done."

William was simply glowing, "Ah well, I used to do this all the time with my dad, but I haven't in years."

Jesus stood looking, no longer smiling, but with a serious look on his face. "Well done, my good and faithful servant."

He fell to his knees and wept. To himself he was thinking, "For so many years I've been waiting and longing to hear those words."

"I know," said Jesus.

William was thinking, "He knows?"

"Yes, I know. How you sacrificed and gave when you hardly had enough money to feed your family, how you were always ready and eager to help someone in need, how you remained faithful to always teach the truth even when all around you others were compromising and bending to the direction of popular culture. Well done."

William could hardly believe his ears. He just wanted to stay here and worship for days and weeks. But then he had a terrifying thought. Jesus knows everything I'm thinking, so what if a wicked thought passes through my mind, a jealous thought, a spiteful thought? Worse yet, what if I have a thought of lust for another woman? I will be so embarrassed!"

"My dear one," said Jesus "you needn't worry. All those sinful thoughts came from your old sinful body, your brain, which inherited a sinful nature from your father, which he inherited from his father. That body is even now being delivered to the funeral home and will soon be buried six feet in the ground."

Anticipating William's next thought Jesus answered, "And even when you were alive on earth, I knew all your struggles, your temptations, your victories, and your failures. And I understood, I was a man myself you know."

"Wow," thought William. "He knew me, yet He loved me."

William was looking at the waterfall and the swirling, ever-changing colors of the mist.

"I made it myself; do you like it?" Jesus said with a grin.

"It's the most beautiful thing I've ever seen. When did you make it?" asked William.

Jesus smiled. "Just now, before you arrived."

William's mouth dropped open. "Just now? You made it just now? Which means you made it just for me? You actually loved me that much?"

"I love you that much," said Jesus.

"Wow," said William. "And all this? The forest and the stream and the deer?"

"And your house, and the rock, and the 57 Chevy. I actually had fun with that – how was the color?" asked Jesus.

"Perfect," William answered.

"Would you like to take a walk?" asked Jesus.

# Walking With Jesus

"I can't believe I'm here with you, walking with you, talking with you, one on one. I imagined a huge throng of people all gathered before your throne, bowing down and worshipping. With so many people I thought that it would be a long time before you got to me. And I would have waited, patiently, even for years, if necessary," said William solemnly.

Jesus stopped and looked him in the eye, "But I couldn't have. I've been longing for this day to be with you."

William wiped a tear from his eye. "But don't you have a lot of people waiting to see you? I've never liked to make people wait on my account."

Jesus smiled. "That's very considerate of you. When I was on the earth, as a human, I was limited as all humans are. I could only be in one place at one time and only talk to one person at a time. Now, I no longer have that limitation."

William nodded, beginning to understand. "So, you can have this same level of intimacy with everyone in Heaven, all at the same time."

"And with those below", added Jesus.

"I have a question," said William, "several in fact. When I was in the garage, and I walked through the door, I know you could do that, after the resurrection that is, you walked through walls and you also ate food."

Jesus nodded. "And I can now, same as then. You're asking if you have your resurrection body, and the answer is 'no.' Let me explain. When you made the decision to go through that door, that was when you died."

"So," asked William, "I could have chosen to stay if I'd wanted to?"

Jesus replied, "You could have stayed, for a while longer. The human will is a powerful thing, but your body was failing fast, and eventually, nature will always win. You chose, wisely, to come here. It was time."

"Is that what they call 'giving up the ghost?'" asked William.

"Yes. Your 'ghost' is another name for your spirit, which means your soul. Your soul passed through to the other side while your body stayed. Think of your body as a tent. You live in it your entire life, be it short or long. When your tent gives way, it dies and decays but your soul and spirit live forever. Actually, your earthly body is in a constant state of decay but when young, new growth outpaces the decay. As you get older the new growth slows down and the decay takes the lead. For every person, their body eventually dies and every soul lives on."

"So every body is subject to sin and every soul is pure?" asked William.

Jesus looked profoundly sad. "Every body is sinful and corrupt, but every soul is not pure. I gave my own life to pay the penalty for sin, for everyone. That day when you got on your knees, humbled yourself, and asked for forgiveness, your soul was saved. Your soul was regenerated, made pure. Sadly, many reject the opportunity to be saved. They can't come here because they are sinful. There is no sin here."

They walked on in silence. Finally, William blurted out, "So this is not my resurrection body?"

"No, it's not even a body, it's a form," Jesus replied.

"What do you mean by 'form'?" asked

William.

"How much do you know about Angels?" Jesus asked.

William grimaced. "Not a whole lot, to tell you the truth."

"Tell me what you know," prodded Jesus.

"Well, when they appear in the Bible they are on a special mission from God, and they appear in human form."

Jesus pointed to him, "There you go, there's your answer, they *appear* in human form, but their natural form is spiritual not physical."

William nodded. "They have white clothes and have a radiant glow about them. They are very powerful; they seem to be kind and wise."

Jesus motioned for him to continue. "They do God's work, some are messengers, some warriors, and some are guardian angels. All those documented in the Bible are male. They appear to have ranks, some with more authority than others. Only three are identified by name: Michael, Gabriel, and Lucifer."

"Very good," said Jesus.

"And Linda said Angels don't marry, so I assume they don't have children. She said we are not Angels but we are *like* Angels. So, what is the difference?" asked William.

Jesus answered, "The main difference is *experience*. Angels were created to worship and know nothing else. You, on the other hand, have witnessed the ravages of sin and have experienced forgiveness."

William nodded. "He who is forgiven much loves much?"

"Yes, that's right. You also understand what it's like to be tempted, to fall, and not want to get back up. You are in a unique position to help the Guardian Angels."

"So, are you going to assign me to a team?" asked William.

Jesus paused. "In due time." They heard an eagle cry and both looked up. Jesus tore a piece of bark from a log and put it over his arm, then He held it up.

# The Eagle

William felt the whoosh of wind on his face as the eagle flapped its wings and landed on Jesus' arm.

"What a magnificent creature!" exclaimed William. "I've always loved nature." (of course, Jesus knew that) "Are all the creatures on earth here too?"

"All and many others you've never seen before." Jesus laughed heartily "And some I haven't created yet."

Jesus moved to a new subject. "So, do you like the form I made for you?" he asked, pointing to his body.

"Very much so, I never looked this good even in my prime," William answered proudly.

Jesus asked him a question: "William, do you see this Eagle? What if I commanded him to walk on the ground and not to fly? And what if I gave him certain clothes to wear to change his appearance and hide his feathers? He would do it of course, if I commanded him, but how do you think it would make him feel?"

"I suppose," said William, "that he would find it very limiting."

"Limiting. A good choice of words. You could also say unnatural," added Jesus. "What if I told you the Angels don't like to take on human form? They find it limiting and unnatural."

"And the others, those like me?" asked William.

"The Saints you mean," Jesus answered. "Many feel the same, but there are also many that use the human form for nostalgic reasons."

"So, we can take on any form we want?" asked William eagerly.

"Within reason, there are some limits even here," answered Jesus with a smile.

William was really excited. "So, I could take on the form of an eagle? And I could fly, I could actually fly?" asked William

Jesus nodded.

"Teach me how," coaxed William.

"All in good time. I need to explain some of the limitations," Jesus answered.

"Limitations. Okay. I know I can't marry. Can I eat?" asked William.

Jesus smiled. "No, not now, but when you get your resurrection body you can."

"When will I get that?" asked William expectantly.

Jesus grinned mischievously. "Why, at the resurrection of course."

"Ok, good enough," thought William. "If Jesus wants me to know more, He will tell me." He was reminded of the times His disciples had asked Him, "When, Lord?"

Jesus, knowing his thoughts, reminded him, "You don't need to worry about time anymore. You will eat again, that is enough for now, and you will marry again. In fact, both will happen together."

Williams's eyes opened wide. He thought he was getting a handle on all this but this was a surprise and a half.

Jesus said, "Do you remember in the Book of Revelation, you received a wedding invitation? It's for a marriage and a feast. It says:

'BLESSED ARE THOSE WHO ARE CALLED TO THE MARRIAGE SUPPER OF THE LAMB!'

William, you and all the other Saints are my bride and I am the bridegroom. It will not be a wedding like the weddings you attended on earth, it will be a hundred times greater."

William had no doubt about that. He thought about that huge wedding feast and how wonderful it would be.

He went on thinking: "I know from First Thessalonians 4 that the 'dead in Christ will rise first,' is that me?"

Jesus nodded. "Your soul and your spirit are alive, obviously, but your old decaying body will one day be resurrected, just as my body was resurrected. Not you only but every Saint of God from the time I was on the earth and also those believers from the times of old."

William whistled, surprised he knew how. "That's a lot of graves. Will the earth be disturbed?"

Jesus grinned, "Let's just say it will shake things up a little."

William laughed, "And then those believers that remain?"

Jesus answered, "As Paul wrote in First Corinthians 15

'BEHOLD, I TELL YOU A MYSTERY: WE SHALL NOT ALL SLEEP, BUT WE SHALL ALL BE CHANGED—'"

William completed the verse:

"IN A MOMENT, IN THE TWINKLING OF AN EYE, AT THE LAST TRUMPET. FOR THE TRUMPET WILL SOUND, AND THE DEAD WILL BE RAISED INCORRUPTIBLE, AND WE SHALL BE CHANGED."

"Amen," Jesus said.

"Amen," agreed William. "That will be a glorious day. Lord, I had many friends on earth, good believers that went on before me, along with my mom and dad, aunts and uncles, and my grandparents. Will I have to wait until the resurrection to see them?"

Jesus put his hand on his shoulder. "My friend, you worry too much. They are all here, and have been anxiously awaiting your arrival."

"They are, that's great. How will I know them? You said their appearance might be different, they might not know me since my appearance is certainly different," asked William earnestly.

"How did you know me?" asked Jesus.

William didn't know.

"My friend," Jesus started.

William noticed. "Did He just call me 'friend'? I thought He did before and now I'm sure of it."

"You are my friend," Jesus confirmed. "Do you remember when Peter, James, and John went with me to the top of the mountain? The one they now call 'The Mount of Transfiguration'?"

William nodded.

Jesus continued, "They saw Moses and Elijah appear before them. Both had lived hundreds of years before their time. How did they know them?"

William was puzzled. "Why, I don't know, did you tell them?"

"No," answered Jesus. "They knew, the same way you knew me, the same way you knew Linda."

"But she appeared to me looking like she did when we first met," argued William.

"Doesn't matter, you'd have still known her," Jesus said.

"You're right, I'd have known her," answered William.

"And my mom and dad, are they well?"

Jesus smiled. "They are here, therefore, they are well. See for yourself."

He turned and saw his mother and father.

"Welcome home, Son," his father said.

"And you too, Dad. And, Mom, you look so wonderful."

"Let me look at you," said his Mom, "You look so handsome." She grabbed hold of his cheek and pinched it harder than was comfortable, but he didn't mind. "In fact," she said, "you look just like Jesus."

"Really?" His eyes welled up with tears as he remembered the verse in First John that said,

"BELOVED, NOW WE ARE CHILDREN OF GOD; AND IT HAS NOT YET BEEN REVEALED WHAT WE SHALL BE, BUT WE KNOW THAT WHEN HE IS REVEALED, WE SHALL BE LIKE HIM, FOR WE SHALL SEE HIM AS HE IS."

He looked around and Jesus was no longer there, but he saw a large group of people approaching. He saw his brother, his sister, his grandparents, many other relatives, friends, and many, many others. They told him how he had encouraged them and many of them said they came to Christ because of him. There were tears of joy. But when he asked about some who were missing there were bitter tears of grief, knowing they had died without hope. There were some that he assumed were saved because they attended church, yet they were lost. His mother took him in her arms and comforted him. Once a mom, always a mom.

"So those that say 'no tears in Heaven' are mistaken?" William asked his mom.

"Not completely mistaken," his mother answered. "Jesus will wipe away all tears, but that day is still far into the future."

William's dad chimed in, "People are prone to take a verse out of context, especially ones that say what they want to hear. It is so important to go back to the beginning of the chapter, or further, to get the context."

William smiled. "I remember a phrase you were fond of. 'When you see a "therefore," you need to go "be-fore" to see what the therefore is there for.'"

They all laughed.

"So, Dad, maybe now you can clear up all those questions we had about the End Times," suggested William.

"Well, Son, being here has cleared some things up, and talking with Brother Paul,"

"Wait, you mean the Apostle Paul? You actually sit and discuss scripture with the Apostle Paul?" asked William.

"Oh yes! Quite frequently. You're welcome to join us if you like," his dad answered.

William was beside himself. "If I'd like? Of course, I would. What days do you meet?"

His dad frowned. "Uh, Son, we don't do days and hours here, but I will get you when it's time, don't worry. Anyway, we are pretty clear on the what, but we're still a little foggy on the when."

"When. That is always the question, isn't it?" said William.

"Are we there yet?" his mom chimed in, "I feel like we are back in our old station wagon with you kids in the back."

# Are We There Yet?

William smiled at his mom and then turned back to his dad. "So, tell me what's next."

"Well, the next major event is The Tribulation. It looms like a hammer over the anvil. All the signs are present, the sharp moral decline, the falling away of the church, the false religions, false christs."

"Dad, the world is really in a terrible state right now, you wouldn't believe the wickedness and the new kinds of sexual perversions that are constantly being invented. And it's not just Hollywood anymore, it's the government, big corporations, the school system, civic leaders, and preachers. All the way down to the neighbors next door. And they are hell-bent on converting all the children over to their way of thinking, to their new 'religion'."

William's dad looked grave. "Son, I know it's hard to believe but things will get even worse until eventually, the whole system will collapse. Out of that chaos, the Antichrist will arise. He will broker a peace treaty between the Jews and the Muslims, all the Jews and all the Muslims, paving the way for the rebuilding of the temple, and the resumption of the temple worship and animal sacrifices. That is a tremendously important event and we need to make note of the day it is signed, for when that happens it will mark the beginning of the seven-year Tribulation Period. It will be a terrible time to be alive on Planet Earth."

A shiver went down William's back as he thought of the antichrist deceiving the whole world, the mark of the beast, and all the death and destruction that was soon to take place. "But the rapture will come first, right? Jesus was just telling me, that the resurrection of every believer that has died will come first, that's what Paul called the 'Dead in Christ', then those that are alive and remain will be 'caught up' to meet Jesus in the air."

William's dad was nodding. "What a privilege for you, Son, to hear those words from our Lord. But did He say when?"

"Well, actually, no."

William's mom spoke up, "Jesus said in

Mark 13:32:

'BUT OF THAT DAY AND HOUR NO ONE KNOWS, NOT EVEN THE ANGELS IN HEAVEN, NOR THE SON, BUT ONLY THE FATHER.'"

William was a little puzzled. "So, The Father knows but Jesus doesn't? How is that possible?"

His dad answered, "I don't know Son, but at the time He said it, He was on earth, in his human body, so the connection with The Father was not the same as it is now."

"That's true", William replied.

"Even now people ask him 'when', and He confirms the information in the scriptures, but He hasn't given us much in the way of new information."

"What does He say?" asked William.

"Watch and Pray."

"That's it?" asked William.

"Yes, but that word 'watch' doesn't mean we are just spectators, it means to 'set a watch, to stand watch, to guard, to be ready to sound the warning,'" his dad explained.

"And more," commented William. "We're

to study, to search the scriptures, to pay attention to information coming to us from all sources."

"Right," his mom said, "and we're to

'ENCOURAGE EACH OTHER ALL THE MORE AS WE SEE THE DAY APPROACHING.'"

"Amen," they all said together, "Amen."

William looked at his mom and dad, the love and happiness they radiated. "I always wondered what the end would be like."

"No Son, not the end, the beginning."

# Epilog

Thank you for reading, and I hope you enjoyed catching a glimpse of the glory of Heaven. I am sooo looking forward to Heaven and I know you are too. It'll be like going on a trip to Hawaii only a million times more wonderful.

But I have to ask you, "Do you have your ticket?" You can't get on an airplane without a ticket and neither can you go to Heaven without one.

Remember in the story how William rejoiced with his loved ones in Heaven, but when he looked around and saw that many were missing, he asked about them and was told "they didn't make it". They wept bitter tears because they were certainly lost forever. They all assumed they would be there, because they went to church, they seemed be true Christians, but the tragedy is they were never ever saved.

The saddest words in all the Bible have to be found in Matthew 7:23 where Jesus says:

"AND THEN I WILL DECLARE TO THEM, 'I NEVER KNEW YOU; DEPART FROM ME, YOU WHO PRACTICE LAWLESSNESS!'"

If you were to die today, and stood before Jesus, and He asked you, "Why should I let you into my Heaven?" what would you tell Him?

Perhaps you'd answer, "I'm a pretty good person." And I'm sure you are, compared to those around us. But unfortunately, God doesn't grade on a curve. In fact the Bible says:

"ALL HAVE SINNED AND FALL SHORT OF THE GLORY OF GOD"

ALL. Everyone. That includes you and me.

In Romans 3:10 it says:

"THERE IS NONE RIGHTEOUS, NO NOT ONE."

Perhaps you'd point to your baptism certificate or your certificate of confirmation. You may even have and ordination certificate stating you are an Ordained Minister. Perhaps you are a Deacon or a Sunday School teacher.

A man named Nicodemus came to Jesus late one night. He was one of the most respected religious teachers in the whole country. Yet Jesus told him

"YOU MUST BE BORN AGAIN."

Think about it, if it were possible in any way for us to earn our salvation by doing something, then it would have been unnecessary for Jesus to die on the cross. When Jesus prayed in the garden, just prior to his arrest and subsequent torture and execution, quite understandably He was in anguish. He prayed to God the Father and asked "Is there any other way? If so let this cup pass before me." But there was no other way. Jesus suffered and died so that we wouldn't have to.

Here's the key: When we stop making excuses, when we are willing to humble ourselves, and freely admit that we are not good people but bad people, terrible even, then God gives us something called "grace". Grace means "unmerited mercy". Unmerited means we didn't earn it or work for it.

In the book of Ephesians, 2:8-9, it says:

"FOR BY GRACE YOU HAVE BEEN SAVED THROUGH FAITH, AND THAT NOT OF YOURSELVES; IT IS THE GIFT OF GOD, NOT OF WORKS, LEST ANYONE SHOULD BOAST."

If we worked for our salvation (our ticket) then surely we would have something to be proud of and most likely we would boast about it.

But God hates boasting and most assuredly hates pride. On the other hand, God loves humbleness. God loves faith. A simple childlike faith. Someone that just believes God. Romans 10:9-10 says:

"IF YOU CONFESS WITH YOUR MOUTH THE LORD JESUS AND BELIEVE IN YOUR HEART THAT GOD HAS RAISED HIM FROM THE DEAD, YOU WILL BE SAVED. FOR WITH THE HEART ONE BELIEVES UNTO RIGHTEOUSNESS, AND WITH THE MOUTH CONFESSION IS MADE UNTO SALVATION."

What does that mean? Let me explain. Do you believe that Jesus died on the cross to pay for our sins? Yes? Do you believe that Jesus rose from the dead? This is the resurrection we celebrate on Easter Sunday. If you do then this demonstrates that you have faith. This makes you a candidate for salvation. To receive this "gift of God" you need only to open your mouth and confess freely and unashamedly "Jesus is Lord of all." Say "Jesus be My Lord." Say "Jesus forgive me for my sins."

My friend, if you really want to go to Heaven, if you are willing to make Jesus the Lord, the ruler of your life, then stop right now. Close your eyes and pray a prayer similar to this: "Jesus come into my heart and save me." Or say "Jesus I am a sinner, please save me." The words are not important, but what is important is the attitude of your heart. Close your eyes right now and pray. If you are already follower of Jesus and have a real day-to-day relationship with Him, then pray a prayer of thanksgiving to your Lord and savior.

Amen! If you prayed that prayer and meant it, you are now a Christian. A follower of Christ.

What's next? Start by praying every day. Simply talk to God. Read your Bible, that's the main way God speaks to us. If you mess up, no let me say *when* you mess up, don't beat yourself up. The Bible makes a promise in First John 1:9

"IF WE CONFESS OUR SINS, HE IS FAITHFUL AND JUST TO FORGIVE US OUR SINS AND TO CLEANSE US FROM ALL UNRIGHTEOUSNESS."

Find a group of Christians you can meet with and encourage each other. Attend church, and participate, get involved. Get to know people. If you don't know anyone at your church either you're not making an effort, or you may be in the wrong church.

Do you have your ticket? Hold it up high. That ticket has one word printed on it: **Jesus**.

Made in the USA
Coppell, TX
14 February 2024

29037808R00039